LI**ON** Lion

Miriam Busch

Illustrated by

Larry Day

Balzer + Bray
An Imprint of HarperCollins*Publishers*

To Larry,
who leaps into
the lion's jaws
with me.
And to Anne,
Laura, and
Christine, who
shine rescue
torches.
—M.B.

To Miriam,
who fills my life
with color
—L.D.

Lion!

ISBN 978-0-06-227104-4

The artist used watercolor, gouache, Wolff pencil, and pencil on Twinrocker handmade watercolor paper to create the illustrations for this book. Typography by Martha Rago. 14 15 16 17 18 SCP 10 9 8 7 6 5 4 3 2 1 ❖ First Edition

Lion!

What are you doing?

Trying to find Lion.
What about you?

I'm looking for lunch.

Lunch?
Care for some grass?

No.
Too snappy.

Snappy?

Ah, I see.
Maybe a mushroom?

**No.
Too prickly!**

Do you
like berries?
Ripe and
delicious.

**No.
Too stinky.**

Hmm. Snappy, prickly, stinky, you say?

How about seeds?

NO.

Well, then.
Flowers?

No!

NO!

No!

Feathers make me sneeze.

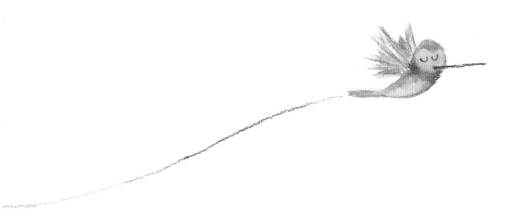

Sneeze? You don't say.

Lion must be very hungry now.
Let's bring him home.

Don't worry, Lion!

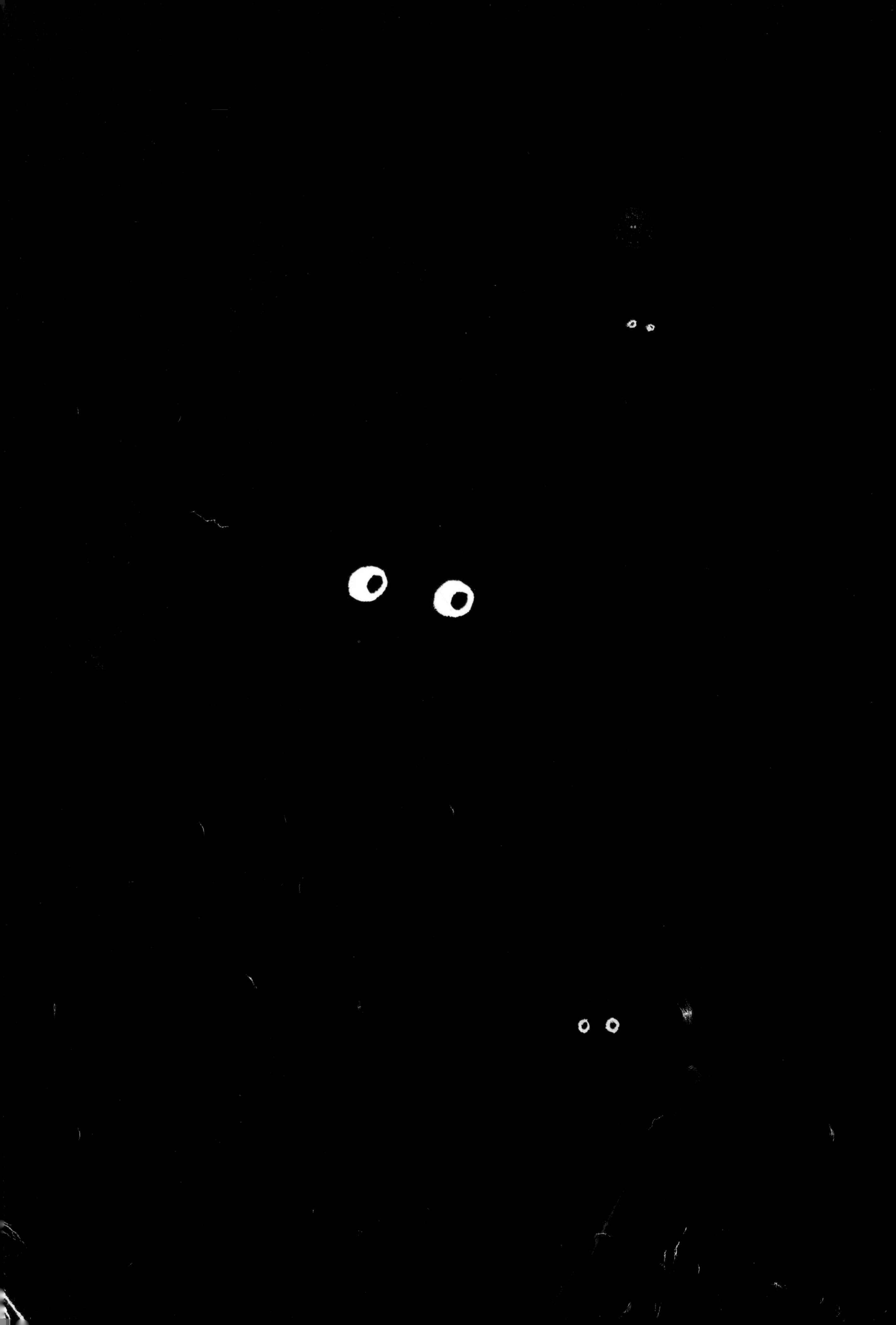

Mew!

There you are, Lion!

Ah...

ahh...

ahhh...

cho

Lion!

Mew!